Pete the Cat

Five Little Bunnies

ISBN 978-0-06-286829-9

The artist used pen and ink, with watercolor and acrylic paint, on
300lb hot press paper to create the illustrations for this book.
19 20 21 22 23   SCP   10 9 8 7 6 5 4 3 2 1
❖
First Edition

Pete the Cat
Five Little Bunnies

by Kimberly & James Dean

HARPER

An Imprint of HarperCollinsPublishers

One night, Pete was bunny-sitting five little bunnies, when all of a sudden . . .

5 little bunnies hopping on the bed,
One fell off and bumped his head.

HOME
SWEET
HOME

Pete called the doctor,
And the doctor said,

"NO MORE
BUNNIES
HOPPING
ON THE BED!"

4 little bunnies hopping on the bed,

One fell off and bumped her head.

Pete called the doctor,
And the doctor said,

"NO MORE BUNNIES HOPPING ON THE BED!"

3 little bunnies hopping on the bed,

One fell off and bumped his head.

Pete called the doctor,
And the doctor said,

"NO MORE
BUNNIES
HOPPING
ON THE BED!"

2 little bunnies hopping on the bed,

One fell off and bumped his head.

Pete called the doctor,
And the doctor said,

1 little bunny hopping on the bed,
One fell off and bumped her head.

Pete called the doctor,
And the doctor said,

So Pete and the five little bunnies
hopped right into bed!